Special thanks to
Linda Chapman

To Julie Sykes for helping so
much – in ALL ways

ORCHARD BOOKS
338 Euston Road, London NW1 3BH
Orchard Books Australia
Level 17/207 Kent Street, Sydney, NSW 2000
A Paperback Original

First published in 2013 by Orchard Books

Text © Hothouse Fiction Limited 2013

Illustrations © Orchard Books 2013

A CIP catalogue record for this book is available
from the British Library.

ISBN 978 1 40832 381 6

1 3 5 7 9 10 8 6 4 2

Printed in Great Britain

Orchard Books is a division of Hachette Children's Books,
an Hachette UK company

www.hachette.co.uk

Series created by Hothouse Fiction

www.hothousefiction.com

Reading Consultant: Prue Goodwin,
lecturer in literacy and children's books

# Midnight Maze

## ROSIE BANKS

ORCHARD

# The Secret Kingdom

# Midnight Maze

# Contents

# Summer Fun

The smell of burgers cooking on the
barbecue drifted across the Honeyvale
School playground. Adults and children
wandered around brightly-coloured stalls
– the lucky dip, the cake stall and the
bouncy castle. Sitting behind the face-
painting table, Summer Hammond put
down her book and sighed happily. She
loved the school fete.

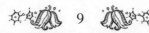

Beside her, her friend Ellie finished painting a tiger face onto Finn, Summer's little brother. "What do you think?" she asked, holding up a mirror.

Finn roared. "I'm the best tiger ever!"

"I've got a tiger joke for you, Finn," Ellie said. "Which day do tigers eat the most people?"

"I don't know! Which day?" asked Finn curiously.

"*Chews*-day!" Ellie grinned.

Finn giggled. Summer shook her head as she laughed. Ellie was always telling

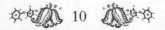

jokes, and some of them were really bad!

"I'm going to have another go at the lucky dip. Thanks, Ellie." Finn jumped up and ran away.

"I love face-painting!" Ellie said happily, pushing her red curls back behind her ears.

"You're brilliant at it." Summer had been reading a fairy tale book while Ellie painted the faces. Now she started to tidy away the brushes. It had been really busy when they first started but the queue had finally quietened down. She checked her watch. "Olivia and Maddie should be coming to swap over with us soon, then we can go and look round the fete ourselves."

"And find Jasmine. I wonder how she's been getting on?" Ellie thought out loud.

Jasmine was their other best friend. She had decided to dress up as a wise woman and tell people's fortunes.

"We'll have to drag her away from fortune-telling for a while," said Summer. "I want to buy some fairy cakes from the cake stall. They look yummy."

"Not as yummy as *real* fairy cakes," said Ellie.

They smiled at each other. "Definitely not!" said Summer. She grinned as she thought about the amazing secret she shared with her two

best friends. They had a magic box that could whisk them away to an enchanted land called the Secret Kingdom. The box had been made by King Merry, the kindly ruler there. When the beautiful kingdom had been in trouble, the box had come into the human world to find the only people that could help – Summer, Ellie and Jasmine!

"Do you remember when we ate fairy cakes that turned us into fairies for a few minutes?" Summer whispered.

Ellie nodded. "And those flying cupcakes we saw at Sugarsweet Bakery that really flew in the air."

Summer sighed longingly. "Oh, I hope Trixi sends us a message in the Magic Box soon. We must go back – King Merry still needs our help."

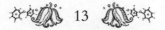

The king's wicked sister, Queen Malice, caused all sorts of problems in the Secret Kingdom. Her most recent evil plan had been to trick King Merry into eating a cursed marshmallow cake, and now the king was slowing turning into a horrible creature called a stink toad. Only a counter-potion made from six rare ingredients could break the spell. Ellie, Summer and Jasmine had found five of the ingredients so far, but time was running out. If King Merry didn't drink the counter-potion by midnight on the night of the Summer Ball, he would be a stink toad for ever.

"King Merry was acting really like a toad when we saw him last," Ellie said anxiously. "I hope he hasn't got any worse."

Summer nodded. She loved the jolly, round king and she hated the thought of him turning into a stink toad. Luckily he didn't realise what was happening because his royal pixie, Trixi, and her wise aunt, Maybelle, had cast a spell to make everyone forget all about the curse, so that no one panicked while Summer, Ellie and Jasmine were busy finding the ingredients for the counter-potion.

"I wonder what the last ingredient will be," said Summer.

Just then, Olivia and Maddie came to take over the face-painting stall and Summer and Ellie quickly stopped talking.

"Thanks for taking over," Ellie said to the other girls.

Summer pushed her book into her bag

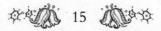

as she and Ellie hurried to find Jasmine's stall. It was a stripy tent with a large notice in swirly letters outside:

*Madame Jasmina Rose. Fortune Teller Extraordinaire.*
*Come inside. If you dare...*

As they reached the tent, a Year Three girl came out. "Oh, wow," she said, looking dazed. "I've got to remember my lucky number is eight so I can have lots of good luck from now on!"

Ellie and Summer giggled and poked their heads into the tent. Jasmine was sitting behind a table. She was wearing a long, colourful skirt and shawl and had a scarf tied round her head, over her long dark hair. She grinned when she saw

them. "Ah, two pretty little girls," she said in a quavering voice, just like an old woman. "Come to hear your fortunes, have you, my sweeties?" She beckoned to them, her dark eyes teasing.

"All right. Tell me my future, Madame Jasmina." Ellie held out her hand.

Jasmine examined it. "Oh, no! What is this?" she exclaimed dramatically. "I see you have a journey to go on! A journey to an exciting place far away!"

17

"Could it be to a *secret kingdom* maybe?" Ellie teased back.

Jasmine chuckled and straightened up. "I hope that's in *all* our futures!"

"Have you got the Magic Box?" Summer asked eagerly.

"Yes. It's in here." Jasmine picked her bag up from under the desk and brought out the box. Its wooden sides were carved with pictures of mermaids and unicorns and there was an oval mirror on the lid surrounded by six green gems. Whenever their friends in the Secret Kingdom wanted to send them a message, the mirror would light up. Summer looked at it, but to her disappointment it wasn't glowing now.

Jasmine stretched. "I've had enough of telling fortunes for now. I want to

go and look round the fete. Come on!"
She pulled off the shawl and long skirt.
Underneath she was wearing shorts and
a sparkly, bright-pink T-shirt. She turned
the sign on the outside of the tent from
'COME IN' to 'BUSY' and then they all
went to look round the stalls.

The girls wandered from stall to stall,
making sure that they saw everything.
They guessed how many sweets there
were in a jar and tried to work out
where treasure was hidden on a map.
Then they went over to where their PE
teacher was showing people how to do
a dance. Five or six girls were standing
on some mats while she told them what
to do.

"Come on! Let's join in!" said Jasmine.
She loved dancing.

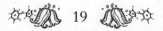

"I'll wait here," said Summer, shyly.
She didn't really like people watching her
perform.

"No, come on!" Jasmine urged.

"It'll be fun," said Ellie.

"O-kay." Summer gave in as her
friends grabbed her hands and pulled her
onto the dance floor.

The PE teacher welcomed them.
"Come and join in! It's easy. You step
to the right then turn around. Step to the
left and then link arms with the person
to your right and swing each other in a
circle. Have a go!"

Ellie was right. It was lots of fun and
Summer soon forgot about the people
watching. Jasmine swung her round
wildly and Summer squealed, her blonde
hair flying.

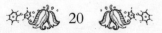

By the time the dance
ended, they were all
tired but happy.

"I'm really
hungry now,"
said Jasmine.
"Let's go
and get some
cakes." But as
she picked up her
bag, she gasped.
Light was spilling out
of the top of her rucksack.
"The Magic Box! It's glowing!"

"Quick! Back to your tent!" said Ellie.

Forgetting all about cakes, they raced
back to Jasmine's fortune-teller tent.
There must be a new message from the
Secret Kingdom!

# A Riddle Solved

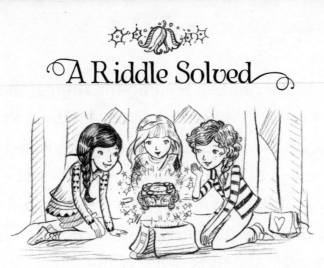

Jasmine, Summer and Ellie pulled the
tent flap firmly closed behind them,
making sure the sign was still turned to
'BUSY'. Summer took the Magic Box
out of the bag. Silver light was streaming
from it and words were swirling up to
the surface of the lid. Ellie read them out:

"Near where pixies learn to fly
Around the trees and way up high,
Find the cottage of a friend
And then this horrid curse will end."

As she finished reading the rhyme, the
lid on the box sprang open. Inside it were
six little compartments each containing
a magical object. There was a special
crystal that controlled the weather and a
tiny bag of glitter dust, with enough left
to grant the girls two wishes.

A fountain of sparkles shot out of the
box and the magical moving map of
the Secret Kingdom rose out of its space.

It floated into the air and unfolded itself, showing the crescent-shaped island spread out below as if they were seeing it through a window. As Summer looked at it she remembered all the wonderful places they'd already visited. She could see smoke puffing from the chimney of Sugarsweet Bakery, stripy bubblebees buzzing round Bubble Volcano and water nymphs waving from the backs of giant water snails as they swam around Clearsplash Waterfall.

"We've got to find a place where pixies learn to fly…" She studied the map.

"We learn things at school," said Jasmine. "Can anyone see any schools?"

"There!" cried Ellie. "What about that?" She pointed to a glade in a wood. There was a small pixie-sized building

made out of shimmering white stone standing in the centre of it. Golden flags waved from its roof and little pixies were swooping through the air around it, riding on all different types of leaves. "The Pixie Flying School!" Ellie said, peering at the small label beside it. "That must be it!"

"But that's not actually where we have to go. The riddle says we've got to look for the cottage of a friend *near* there," Summer pointed out. She noticed a tiny little house nestling in the roots of an oak tree. It had a thatched roof, and pink roses covered its white walls. There was a wishing well in the garden and beds of bright wild flowers all around. The label was in very small writing. "Rose Cottage," Summer read out. "Maybe

that's where we're supposed to go?"

"I'm not sure," said Jasmine. "The riddle said it was the cottage of a *friend*, but I don't know who lives there."

"It must belong to a pixie because it's so small," Summer reasoned. "So, which pixies do we know? Of course!" she gasped suddenly. "It must be Trixi's aunt, Maybelle! Rose Cottage could be where she lives!"

"I bet you're right!" said Ellie.

"Let's try!" said Jasmine. They all placed their hands on the box. "The answer to the riddle is Rose Cottage," they chanted excitedly.

There was a bright flash and a ball of green light shot out of the box and whooshed round their heads. They heard a merry giggle as the ball changed into

a green leaf with a pixie standing on it, holding her arms out as if she was surfing on the sea. She was wearing a long midnight-blue ball dress, and her messy blonde hair peeked out from under a pretty hat made from a bluebell.

"Greetings from the Secret Kingdom!" she cried, whizzing in between them on her leaf.

"Trixi!" the girls cried in delight.

Trixi zoomed over to each girl in turn and kissed them lightly on the nose. "It's lovely to see you all again. I'm glad

you got my message. It's the Summer
Ball tonight. King Merry *must* drink the
counter-potion before midnight or he'll
be a toad for ever."

"But we've still got to find the last
ingredient," said Summer anxiously.
"Will we have enough time?"

Trixi smiled. "Oh, yes! The last
ingredient is a single piece of the feather
from the phoenix that helped the first
ever pixies learn to fly using leaves.
The feather is usually kept in a glass
cabinet at the pixie flying school, so
Aunt Maybelle has already got it! She's
finishing the counter-potion now, and as
soon as it is ready we can all take it to
King Merry."

"And when he drinks it, he'll be
cured?" asked Ellie.

Trixi gave a happy twirl on her leaf. "Yes! And then we can celebrate at the Summer Ball!"

"How is King Merry?" Summer asked.

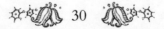

"Very toad-like." Trixi frowned. "He croaks all the time and he keeps eating flies. The sooner he drinks the potion the better."

"Then what are we waiting for?" said Jasmine, her brown eyes shining. "Aunt Maybelle's cottage, here we come!"

# Rose Cottage

Trixi tapped her pixie ring and called out a spell:

"Off to Rose Cottage as pixies small,
To save King Merry before the ball."

A cloud of sparkles shot out of the ring and swirled around the girls. They spun round in the air until Summer suddenly felt something under her feet. It felt like they were flying. She opened her eyes and as the sparkles cleared she gasped when she saw Trixi next to her.

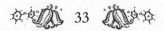

"Trixi! We're on your leaf!" Summer cried. She felt herself wobble and reached out her arms to balance herself.

Trixi grinned. "Do you like it?"

"Oh, yes!" cried Jasmine. They were all the same size as Trixi now and the leaf was soaring over the Secret Kingdom through the cornflower-blue sky.

Ellie sat down shakily. She didn't like heights! "How far have we got to go?" she gulped, not daring to look over the edge of the leaf.

"Don't worry. We'll be down on the ground soon," said Trixi.

Jasmine saw tiaras sparkling on Ellie and Summer's heads, and reached up to touch the one in her own dark hair. She felt a rush of happiness. Whenever the girls arrived in the Secret Kingdom, special tiaras appeared on their heads so that everyone would know they were visitors from the Other Realm, and Very Important Friends of King Merry. "Oh, this is so much fun! And look! Trixi, is that the school?"

"Yes," said Trixi.

Jasmine and Summer looked down at the glittering school. Now they were pixie-sized it looked massive. The golden roof shone in the sunshine, and purple flags embroidered with gold leaves flew

from each corner. The four sides of the building surrounded a large square of emerald-green grass where lots of young pixies were playing and practising flying on green leaves. They all had on dresses in different colours of the rainbow, some wore cute hats made out of petals, and others had flowers woven into their hair. It looked like the most amazing place to go to school!

"Can we go there and visit?" Jasmine asked eagerly.

"Maybe another day," said Trixi. "But right now we have to get to Rose Cottage."

They swooped down towards the nearby cottage. Just like they'd seen through the map, it was surrounded by a little white fence and had pink roses scrambling over its walls and round its bright blue door. A cloud of tiny butterflies fluttered around the wild flowers in the garden. The kitchen window was open and as the leaf landed safely on the ground, the girls could hear a silvery voice saying:

"Pixie magic, weave a spell.
Stop the curse, make King Merry well."

Trixi jumped off the leaf. "Aunt Maybelle! I've brought some visitors!"

A grey-haired, straight-backed pixie with wise blue eyes came to the window. "That's lovely, Trixi, dear, but I am rather busy right now. I…" She broke off. "Oh, glitter and sparkles! It's our friends from the Other Realm!"

Trixi beamed. "They've come to help me take the potion to King Merry."

"Will it really work?" Summer asked the older pixie.

"Oh, yes, my dear," Aunt Maybelle assured her. "So long as the king drinks it before midnight. Now, please – come in!"

The cottage had jars of flowers everywhere and bright rugs on the floor. In the kitchen a shimmering liquid was

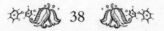

bubbling in a pot on the stove. "Is that the counter-potion?" Ellie asked.

"Yes, I've already put in the bubblebee honeycomb, the silverspun sugar and the book bud," said Aunt Maybelle.

"And here are the other ingredients," said Jasmine, going over to the table. "Dream dust!" she said, holding up a bag of glittering dust.

Summer pictured the gentle dragons who flew around the kingdom helping people sleep by sprinkling magical dream dust on them. "I loved meeting the dragons in Dream Dale."

"Me too. And there's the healing water we collected from Clearsplash Waterfall," Ellie said, pointing to a small silver flask.

"You did so well to get it. And this is the last ingredient," smiled Aunt Maybelle. She carefully took a golden feather from the top pocket of her dress. It glowed, filling the kitchen with light.

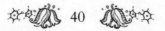

"The phoenix feather!" breathed Trixi in awe. "I've heard about it but I've never seen it before."

"We just need one little piece,' said Aunt Maybelle. She carefully cut off a single frond of feather with some sharp silver scissors and placed it in the pot with the other ingredients. "Now, why don't we all finish the potion together? Summer, please can you add the dream dust while Trixi stirs?"

Summer eagerly picked up the little bag and sprinkled the glittering dust into the potion. As Trixi stirred it in, rainbow-coloured lights swirled over the surface.

"Ellie, could you add the healing water?" Aunt Maybelle said softly.

Ellie took the stopper out of the flask and added the crystal-clear water.

She held her breath as the potion turned a shimmering silver.

"And finally, Jasmine," Aunt Maybelle said. "Will you please add the piece of phoenix feather after I have said the spell?"

Jasmine nodded and carefully picked up the tiny strand of phoenix feather. Aunt Maybelle murmured the spell.

*"Magic objects, hard to find,*
*Mix together, curse unbind.*
*Counter-potion, once complete,*
*Bring about the queen's defeat."*

On the last word, Jasmine dropped the feather in and gold and silver sparks whooshed up from the pot and hit the ceiling.

"Is that supposed to happen?"
exclaimed Summer.

Aunt Maybelle smiled. "Oh, yes. Don't
worry. Now, let's see." She took the pot
off the heat and held it out so they could
all see inside. The potion had reduced
to just a couple of golden spoonfuls.
"Perfect! The counter-potion is complete.

Let's put it in a bottle and you can take it to the palace. All King Merry needs to do is drink one drop and then the curse will be lifted before he turns completely into a toad."

"Oh, no, it won't!" A massive leathery grey face peered in at the window. The girls jumped back. It was a Storm Sprite, one of Queen Malice's  servants. He had a pointed nose and wisps of grey hair and they could hear his bat-like wings flapping on his back. Storm Sprites looked scary enough when the girls were their normal size, but now they were so tiny he looked terrifying! "I've just come from the Enchanted

Palace and you're too late!" the Storm Sprite crowed.

"Go away, you horrible creature!" snapped Aunt Maybelle. She pointed her pixie ring bravely at him. "If you don't, I'll turn you into a pretty bluebird."

The Storm Sprite looked alarmed. "Don't do that! All right, I'll go!"

"Wait!" said Jasmine suddenly. "What did you mean? About King Merry?"

A mean look lit up the sprite's eyes. "You're too late with that stupid potion. King Merry has just turned completely into a stink toad! He's as stinky and toady as a stink toad can be. You can do what you like...but Queen Malice has already won!" Cackling with laughter, he flapped his leathery wings and raced away.

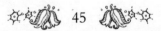

# Race Against Time

"But the ball hasn't even started yet!" Ellie gasped.

Trixi's eyes filled with tears. "Poor King Merry!"

Summer hugged her.

"Don't fret, Trixi dear," Aunt Maybelle said calmly. "King Merry might be a toad, but we can still cure him. So long as he drinks the potion before midnight, he'll change back to his old self. Queen Malice hasn't won yet."

"And she's not going to. We'll make sure he gets the potion safely!" said Ellie.

Jasmine nodded. "Can you magic us to the palace, Trixi?"

Trixi nodded. "Of course I can. You're right. We *can* save him still."

Maybelle spooned a little of the potion into a  crystal bottle and put a cork stopper in. "Here you are."

"There isn't much there," Summer said anxiously. "Is it enough?"

"Oh, yes. All he needs is a single drop." Maybelle handed Ellie the bottle. "Travel safely, my dears. I'll get changed for the ball and then join you at the palace."

Trixi tapped her magic pixie ring and the girls felt themselves being whisked away.

They landed in the middle of a lawn

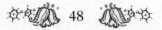

but they were so small
that the grass came
up above their
heads so it was
more like being
in a jungle!
Standing on
tiptoe, Jasmine
saw that they
were in the
palace gardens.
Twinkle-twinkle
bunting hung from every

tree and the brightly coloured rainbow
slide in the pond was shining in the rays
of the late afternoon sun. Elves dressed in
black coats and long white gloves were
putting up more twinkle-twinkle bunting
in the hedges of the palace maze.

"They're setting up for the Summer Ball," explained Trixi. "I wonder where King Merry is?"

"Maybe you should change us back to our normal size first, Trixi," gasped Jasmine, jumping out of the way as an elf almost trod on her.

"Good idea!" Trixi tapped her ring and chanted:

*"Back to human size you go.*
*Ellie, Summer, Jasmine – grow!"*

The girls shot back to their normal heights. "Now, where can King Merry be?" said Trixi. "He likes the palace kitchens. Maybe he's there."

They went inside to the enormous kitchens where brownies were baking

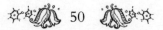

and cooking. Delicious
rainbow jellies
wobbled in great
towers and iced
fairy cakes with
delicate sugar wings
flew around in the air.

"Bobbins!" called Trixi,
spotting the head butler picking up a
tray of giant iced cookies in the shape of
unicorns and mermaids. "Have you seen
King Merry?"

"No, I'm sorry, Trixi, I haven't," the
butler said, shaking his head. He smiled
at the girls. "But it's lovely to see our
honoured visitors again."

"It's lovely to see you too, Bobbins,"
said Summer. "We must find King Merry
though."

"What about the ballroom?" Summer suggested. "King Merry loves sitting on his snuggly throne there." They tried the ballroom next. It had peacock-blue walls and a high domed ceiling covered with beautiful painted murals. There were lots of windows framed by golden curtains and at one end were doors that opened onto the gardens. Glittering chandeliers hung down from the ceiling and the tables were piled high with delicious food and decorated with flowers, but King Merry's throne was empty.

"Oh, where is he?" asked Trixi.

Ellie looked thoughtful. "Hmm. We keep looking in places he liked when he was a person, but he's a stink toad now." She turned to Summer. "You know loads about animals, Summer. What sort of

52

places do *toads* like?"

"Well, toads in our world usually like damp places," said Summer.

"Stink toads do too!" said Trixi. "The damper and smellier the better."

"Where's the dampest, smelliest place in the palace?" said Jasmine.

Trixi frowned. "Well, there isn't anywhere smelly in the Secret Kingdom, but it's very wet around the palace pond."

"Let's look there!" said Jasmine.

They ran back outside. The pond was shining in the sun. Its surface was covered with lily pads and ducks were swimming around in it. The rainbow slide glowed in multi-colours as it plunged into the water. It was a magic slide – sliding down it could take you

anywhere you wanted to go in the Secret Kingdom.

"Are you here, King Merry?' called Ellie cautiously.

"RIBBIT!" They all jumped.

"There!" gasped Summer, pointing to a space in between two rocks at the side of the pond. A stink toad was snapping out its long tongue, catching flies.

Just then Ellie spotted a small gold crown perched lopsidedly on the toad's head. She pointed at it. "It's got a crown. And look—" She pointed at a pair of tiny half-moon shaped glasses perched on the toad's nose. "King Merry's glasses! It *must* be him!"

"Poor King Merry," said Summer, feeling sorry for the cursed king.

"Don't worry, we're about to help

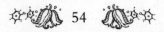

him," said Jasmine. "All we need to do is give him a drop of the potion."

"Who's going to pick him up?" Ellie asked.

"I will." Summer offered. She approached the boulders. "King Merry?" she said softly. "Is that you?"

The toad put its head on one side and gave a loud "RIBBIT!"

He might be King Merry but he smelled just as horrible as any normal stink toad. Summer screwed up her nose and reached out for him. "Come here, King Merry. We just need you to drink a drop of potion…"

"STOP!"

They all swung round and gasped.

"Queen Malice!" Trixi squealed.

A scrawny woman was climbing out of the pond, water dripping off her. There was a spiky crown on her frizzy black hair and in one hand she held a black staff with a thunderbolt on top.

Summer felt her stomach turn a
somersault.

"Did you think I would really let you
stop me?" Queen Malice hissed. As she
hauled herself up the slide, the rainbow
stripes turned to shades of grey under her
touch. "You will not break my curse.
This kingdom will be mine!"

"It won't!" said Jasmine bravely.
"We've got the counter-potion *and*
we've found King Merry!"

"Ha! That's what you think!" Queen
Malice brandished her staff and screamed
out a spell:

> "Stink toads arrive as a disguise
> Hide my brother from meddling eyes!"

There was a thunderclap. The sky

instantly darkened. Trixi shrieked and zoomed about on her leaf in a panic as suddenly lots and lots of stink toads started falling out of the sky!

The girls screamed too as the slimy, smelly toads rained down around them.

"Help!" cried Summer, ducking.

"Quick!" cried Jasmine, dragging the others under the branches of a nearby candyfloss tree.

"Keep an eye on King Merry!" called Ellie anxiously as Trixi zoomed in beside them.

But it was hard to see through the falling toads. There were hundreds of stink toads! Thousands! They landed with little bumps and then started hopping around, croaking happily. The stench of rotten eggs filled the air.

Summer peered at the pond. The King Merry toad had hopped away and joined the others. "We've lost King Merry!" she cried.

Queen Malice cackled as she slid down the slide and vanished. "You'll never find him now!" Her voice echoed back to them. "The Secret Kingdom is going to be mine – all mine!"

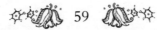

# Follow That Toad!

"We've got to find King Merry!" said Ellie.

"Look for the one with the crown," Summer told them. "He must be here somewhere!"

The garden was in chaos. There were stink toads everywhere, hopping around, croaking and glaring. Storm Sprites were swooping down from the skies too, their beady eyes shining with glee as they landed in the palace gardens.

The girls looked around desperately at the sea of toads.

"This is impossible!" groaned Trixi.

"Wait a minute. Look over there!" Jasmine pointed. A stink toad wearing a crown was hopping into the palace. "There he is!"

"Follow that toad!" Ellie whooped.

Dodging the other toads and holding their noses, the girls raced towards the palace with Trixi flying beside them.

They tumbled in through the open doors into the ballroom. The elf butlers were all running about in a panic and the brownies in the band were waving their musical instruments. There were toads hopping everywhere. Some were on the tables, gobbling up the marshmallow cakes and frosted cherries that had been put out for the guests, others were jumping all over the dance floor. Jasmine snatched up a cupcake before a toad could gobble it whole. There was no sign of the King Merry toad though.

Just then there was a loud knocking at the door. "The guests are here!" cried Bobbins, the head butler, his face pale.

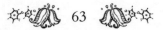

"What are we going to do?" He turned
to the girls. "Please can you help?"

"But we've got to find King Merry,"
Ellie said.

There was a flash of light. "Maybe
I can help instead!" Aunt Maybelle
appeared in the air beside Trixi. She was
wearing an emerald-green
ball dress and her hair
was piled up in an
elegant bun. She was
flying on a golden
leaf, its edges dotted
with tiny sparkling
gems. "Leave the toads
and the guests to me.
You girls find King Merry."

"Thank you, Aunt Maybelle!"
Ellie gasped.

Suddenly, Jasmine gave a squeal. "There he is!" The King Merry toad was leaping back through the ballroom doors and out into the garden.

"King Merry! Come back!" Ellie cried as they raced after him.

But the toad didn't stop. He hopped under an archway made out of a hedge. "Oh, no!" said Trixi in alarm. "That's the entrance to the palace maze. People  have been lost in there for days!"

The girls looked up at the tall, bushy hedge. The light inside the maze was dark and dreary, even with the twinkle-twinkle bunting hanging around the entrance.

"We've got to follow him," Jasmine said bravely. "If we all hold hands we won't lose each other."

The girls stepped into the dim pathway, with Trixi flying overhead on her leaf. "King Merry!" Jasmine called suddenly, making the others jump.

Just then Ellie saw a flash of gold as a toad disappeared round a corner. "Quick!" she cried, racing after it.

Summer and Jasmine followed Ellie as she ran after the troublesome toad. "Left, right, left, left," Jasmine chanted to herself, trying to remember the twists and turns of the maze as she ran along.

Ellie turned around another corner and skidded to a halt so fast that the others almost bumped into her.

"King Merry!" Summer breathed. They

were in a clearing right in the middle
of the maze. The toad with the golden
crown was sitting at a corner where
the maze split off into two different
directions, looking from one to another
as if he was deciding which way to go.
"Ribbit," he said to them mournfully.

Just then Jasmine remembered the cupcake she'd picked up earlier. She'd put it in her pocket as she ran, but now she brought it out. "Here, King Merry," she said, slowly placing it on the ground in front of her. "Come on, King Merry, come and eat the tasty cupcake."

They all held their breath.

The toad hopped greedily up to the cake. Ellie quickly shook the potion on top of it, making sure that she used every last drop. The toad gave another ribbit, and started gobbling it all up.

"We've done it!" Jasmine hugged Ellie and Summer. "King Merry should change back any minute!"

They all stared at the toad. But nothing happened.

"King Merry!" called Ellie.

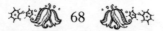

The toad looked at them. "RIBBIT!"

"I don't understand," said Trixi in confusion. "The potion should have worked by now."

"Come on, King Merry – change!" begged Jasmine.

"It's not midnight yet, it should have worked." Ellie cried.

"Oh, poor King Merry," said Summer, her eyes filling with tears. "Is he going to be a stink toad for ever?"

"HAHAHAHA!" A sneering cackle rang out behind them. Queen Malice appeared in the middle of the maze, holding a toad with a gold crown on its head. "You were looking for the king, I believe?" she said, holding up the toad in her arms.

"That's not King Merry!" said Jasmine,

looking back at the toad that was
still munching the cake. "*This* is King
Merry!"

But Summer was staring at the toad in
the queen's arms. "No,
she's right," she said
in horror. "That
toad she's holding
has King Merry's
glasses!" The
others looked
and saw that
the toad was
wearing a pair of
half-moon-shaped
glasses, exactly the
same as the kindly king's.

"But this one had his crown," Ellie said
in confusion.

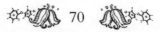

Queen Malice sniggered. "Look around!"

The girls and Trixi swung round. The Storm Sprites were flying overhead with armfuls of matching crowns, putting one on every stink toad.

The sprites chortled. "Queen Malice tricked you! She's so clever! You're as stupid as slime slugs."

Summer couldn't bear it. "We've given the counter-potion to the wrong toad!"

Ellie looked at the empty bottle in her hand in dismay.

"I'm afraid your little plan has gone wrong," said Queen Malice smugly. "Thanks to you girls," she said as she patted the toad in her arms, "my dear brother is going to be a stink toad for ever!"

# Queen Malice's Rules

"RIBBIT!" the King Merry toad protested, as Queen Malice turned and pointed her thunderbolt staff at the palace.

"Glitter and gold now disappear
Leave mud and mess, darkness and fear!"

There was a loud bang and then a thick plume of black smoke shot from

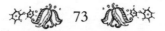

the end of the queen's staff and streamed towards the ballroom. With another flash, Malice disappeared.

"After her!" Ellie yelled.

"But which way is the way out?" Summer asked.

"Trixi, can you magic us back to the palace?" Ellie asked.

Trixi shook her head. "The maze is enchanted so that no one can use magic to cheat. My pixie ring won't work in here. Oh, what are we going to do?"

Ellie and Summer looked around hopelessly. It was starting to get dark, and every pathway looked exactly the same.

But Jasmine had her eyes shut and she was murmuring under her breath. "Left, right, left, left…" she muttered.

"Are you okay, Jasmine?" Summer asked her anxiously.

Jasmine just nodded. "Right, right, left…" she muttered. Ellie and Summer shrugged at each other.

"I think I've got it," Jasmine said in a flash. "But I've got to concentrate. Come on!" She took off down the right-hand path.

Summer and Ellie followed their friend as she raced through the dark bushy corridors of the maze, muttering as she went.

The maze got darker and scarier as the night fell, and soon Summer could barely see where she was going. Her heart started beating fast as she thought about all the people that had been lost in the twists and turns of the maze. She hoped

Jasmine knew where she was going!
Summer focused her eyes on her friends
and followed as quickly as she could.
But as they got to the next corner,
Jasmine stopped. She looked from left
to right, then shook her head. "I don't
know which way to go."

"I do!" Ellie cried. "Look, there's the
twinkle-twinkle bunting the elves were

putting up earlier!" She pointed up ahead to where the sparkly lights were shining brightly.

"Let's go!" Trixi cried, flying her leaf out into the palace gardens.

"Well done, Jasmine," Summer flung her arms around her friend and gave her a big hug. "And Ellie too!"

Jasmine grinned, but then looked at the dark sky anxiously. "Come on!" she said. "It can't be long before midnight, and we have to stop Queen Malice."

They ran to the ballroom and peered in the doorway. Queen Malice was standing in the middle of the room, cackling triumphantly as thick black smoke swirled around, changing everything it touched. The guests cried out in panic as King Merry's beautiful

golden throne turned into a twisted
metal chair with large spikes, the golden
curtains transformed to cobwebs and the
dance floor became a muddy swamp.

"Oh, no!" breathed Jasmine. Flies
swooped in from outside and buzzed
above the swamp, and the stink toads
hopped into it in glee. A grey shadow
spread out from the base of the black
throne, climbing up the walls and over
the ceiling, creeping over the beautiful
room. All around, pixies swooped about
in a panic and the elves, imps and
brownies huddled together in fear.

"This is *my* palace now!" Queen
Malice declared as her Storm Sprites
flapped overhead and landed on King
Merry's throne. "I am the ruler of the
Secret Kingdom and you are all my

subjects!" She pointed her staff at the guests and their beautiful clothes all turned to rags.

"Stop it!" whinnied one of the unicorns bravely, stamping her hoof. "Where is King Merry? He will never allow this."

"Oh, won't he? Well, look closely…"
The queen held the toad up. "*This* is
your wonderful king!"

All of the guests gasped in horror.

"It can't be true!" cried Bobbins. He
turned to Trixi. "It's just a trick, isn't it?"

Trixi shook her head, tears welling
in her big blue eyes. "No. I'm afraid
that toad really is King Merry." A tear
trickled off the end of her nose.

"So, what do you think now, brother?"
sneered Queen Malice to the toad.

He struggled in her hands.

"This is awful!" Jasmine hissed.

"We've got to do something!"
whispered Summer.

Ellie nodded. "We can't just stand
here and let Queen Malice take over the
kingdom."

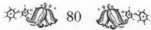

"We've still got a chance," said Jasmine, her thoughts whirring. "If we can rescue the king before midnight then we can still turn him back."

"But there isn't any potion left," Ellie said, taking out the empty bottle.

They all racked their brains. What were they going to do?

"It's...it's all over!" Trixi said in despair. "Queen Malice really has won this time."

"Hang on," said Jasmine. "We might not have any potion *here*, but there is some more at Aunt Maybelle's cottage. Can't you magic it here, Trixi?"

Trixi's eyes widened. "I could try. If I can just think of a spell..." She frowned for a moment. "Got it!" She tapped her ring.

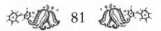

*"Counter-potion, come to me..."*

"SILENCE!" Queen Malice shrieked above the noise of the guests.

She held up her staff so threateningly that everyone, even Trixi, fell quiet. The only sound was the stink toads croaking as they splashed in the mud and caught flies with their long tongues.

"Now I am your queen, things are going to change," Queen Malice snarled. "My spell is already taking over the palace. It will spread across the whole kingdom until there is no more happiness anywhere."

There were gasps of horror.

Summer felt sick. Jasmine and Ellie looked equally worried.

"And there shall be new rules from

now on," the queen went on. "Rule
number one: there will be NO fun!"

"No fun?" whimpered an imp.

Queen Malice sat down on King
Merry's throne with the toady king on
her lap. She laughed above his warty
head. "No fun at all! Rule number two:
there will be no dancing and no music
and certainly no parties!
Rule number three,
you will all just eat
bread and water.
Only my sprites
and I will be
allowed cake!"

The Storm Sprites
whooped.

"And rule
number four:

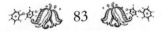

no one may use magic without my permission. Not to make or conjure things or help anybody. Anyone who does magic will be banished from the kingdom for ever!"

Jasmine felt desperate. They *had* to get the potion – but if Trixi conjured it she'd be banished for ever. She looked at the little pixie, who raised her chin bravely.

"If we don't bring King Merry back, the Secret Kingdom will be so horrible that I won't mind being banished," she whispered.

Summer smiled at the brave little pixie.

As the Storm Sprites gave another cheer, Ellie whispered to Trixi, "Now's our chance. Say your spell while the Storm Sprites are making so much noise!"

Trixi quickly tapped her pixie ring and whispered the words:

"Counter-potion, come to me
Fill this bottle, full as can be."

With a faint popping sound, the little glass bottle slowly filled up.

"We've got it!" breathed Summer. "Well done, Trixi!"

"But how do we get it to King Merry?" said Ellie.

"We need to distract Queen Malice," said Jasmine. "Trixi, you and I can do that. Summer, you and Ellie try and get to King Merry and make him drink the potion. Just a drop will do, remember."

"Okay," Summer gulped. She didn't like the idea of running up and grabbing

King Merry right in front of Queen Malice and the Storm Sprites – but she would do it to try and save him and the Secret Kingdom.

"Right!" Jasmine took the bottle and handed it to Ellie. "Here we go!" She marched into the ballroom and lifted her chin. "Queen Malice! I want a word with you!" she shouted.

The Storm Sprites fell silent and the queen gave a cruel laugh. "You? You meddling girl!" Her eyes grew even harder. "I've just thought of another rule: no visitors from the Other Realm shall be allowed into the Secret Kingdom! Leave now!"

"No! Your rules are mean!" Jasmine declared. Everyone drew in their breath. "No one should listen to you. King

Merry should be the ruler. Even as a
stink toad he's a million times better than
you, you…you…great big stick insect!"

"Quick!" Ellie hissed to Summer. The
two of them had been so busy watching
Jasmine in awe that they had almost
forgotten their part of the plan!

"What?" Malice shrieked. She jumped
off the throne, threw King Merry down
on the seat and stormed towards Jasmine.
The Storm Sprites on the back of the
throne watched eagerly.

Summer and Ellie crept towards the
throne as fast as they dared. No one was
looking at them.

"I'll make you sorry you said that!"
Queen Malice hissed, raising her staff.
"If you like stink toads so much then see
how you like BEING one!"

"Stop right there!" Trixi exclaimed. She zoomed in front of the queen's nose like a little rocket, making her blink. "If you hurt Jasmine, I'll cast a spell on you!"

"A spell?" Queen Malice's dark eyes almost popped out of her head. "What sort of spell could *you* do that would stop *me*? Out of my way!" She swiped at Trixi with her staff. Trixi dodged.

"Leave her alone!" cried Jasmine.

Ellie and Summer crouched low so the Storm Sprites wouldn't notice them and crept closer and closer to the throne on their hands and knees. "Now!" hissed Ellie.

Summer leapt up and grabbed the king. He gave a croak of surprise. "It's all right," Summer whispered as Ellie pulled the stopper from the bottle.

But it was too late. King Merry's croak had made one of the sprites look down. "Queen Malice, look!" he shrieked. "Those other girls have got the king!"

"STOP THEM!" yelled the queen.

The Storm Sprites dived towards the girls. The leader swiped at Ellie with his bony fingers. She ducked and the bottle flew out of her hands.

"No!" cried all three girls as it shot high into the air. They watched as it spun slowly in the sky. For a moment it seemed to hang there and then it tumbled to the ground – spilling the precious potion everywhere!

# Strong Magic

Queen Malice screamed with laughter as the potion spattered down onto the floor. "So, you thought you could stop me, did you? Well, you were wrong. You've lost! I've won! I—"

King Merry's long tongue suddenly shot out and caught a drop of the potion as it fell to the ground. With a croak he swallowed.

"NOOOOOOOO!" Queen Malice shrieked.

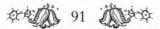

"Yes!" Jasmine yelled, jumping up and down.

Trixi squealed in delight. Ellie and Summer grabbed each other's arms. Would the king change back?

"What time is it?" Malice screamed. "It's midnight if I say it is! Start the countdown or I'll turn you all into flies!" She pointed her staff at the brownie band.

The brownies reluctantly started counting. "Five...four...three..."

Everyone else was staring at King Merry. Had the potion worked in time?

All of a sudden the toad hopped onto his throne and started to swell. For a moment the toad seemed to stretch in all directions like a rubber toy and then suddenly, with a faint pop, he turned

back into the round, tubby king with curly white hair and beard, his half-moon spectacles perched on his nose and his crown sitting wonkily on his head!

"King Merry!" the girls and Trixi exclaimed in delight.

The king blinked as if he couldn't believe it. "You…you saved me!"

Trixi swooped around King Merry's head. "You're back to normal!"

"Not quite normal!" King Merry drew himself up to his full height and glared at his sister. "I am VERY angry and that is *not* normal for me!" The girls stared. King Merry was usually so jolly and happy, but now he looked furious.

"Sister! I have had enough of you!" he bellowed. "First you try and turn me into a stink toad, then you wreck my palace and cast a wicked spell over the whole land. You have gone too far!" Pushing up his sleeves, he pulled out a dusty old book from a pocket inside his long robes.

The queen's face turned pale as her dark eyes fell on the book.

Trixi laughed in delight. "The Secret Spellbook!" she grinned.

"No!" Queen Malice hissed. "You can't use that! That spellbook is too powerful."

"Yes," King Merry nodded. "And I'm going to use it to send you and your Storm Sprites and all the stink toads to the Troll Territories to think about what you have done."

"Nooooo!" Queen Malice wailed, cowering behind her sprites.

King Merry opened the book and a cloud of glitter filled the air. Then he chanted:

*"Secret Spellbook, cast a spell,*
*To make the kingdom safe and well..."*

The book started to shimmer with powerful magic.

"With these words I make it so..."

"I'll get you back for this!" the queen shrieked. "You'll pay for this, brother—"

"To the Troll Territories you must GO!"

King Merry finished, closing the book with a snap.

There was a purple flash and Queen Malice's voice faded away as she vanished – along with all her Storm Sprites and the stink toads.

There was a moment of silence and then everyone in the ballroom started cheering.

"King Merry, that was amazing!"
cried Jasmine, excitedly.

"You were brilliant!" said Ellie.

"Are you all right, King Merry?" asked
Summer in concern.

The king blinked and rubbed his eyes.
"Gosh, crowns and sceptres," he said,
swaying slightly. "I'd forgotten how tired
I always feel when I use the spellbook.
It's no wonder I don't do it very often."

He swayed again. Jasmine and Ellie
grabbed his arms to help him stay
upright.

"Thank you, my dears," he said
gratefully. "Oh, dear. I could really do
with sitting down."

The girls helped him sit down on the
throne, and Trixi magicked him up
a glass of water. Everyone else in the

ballroom was talking all at once.

"Ah, Aunt Maybelle," said the king as he spotted her in the ballroom. "I think I probably have you to thank for the counter-potion."

"Well, I couldn't have made it if the girls and Trixi hadn't found all the ingredients for me," Aunt Maybelle said, smiling at the girls. "They've been wonderful!"

"Trixi was so brave," Summer told the king, making the little pixie blush bright pink.

"We're just glad you're back to normal, King Merry," said Ellie.

"I may be, but my kingdom isn't!" said King Merry anxiously, as he looked around at the dirty, muddy ballroom and his black spiky throne. He shook his

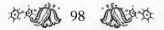

head. "The Summer Ball is completely
ruined and the Secret Kingdom is under
a terrible spell."

Jasmine ran to the window. Outside
there was a horrible scene. All the flowers
had wilted and the grass shrivelled up,
the leaves had dropped from the trees
and everywhere had turned grey. "Is
the spell really going to spread over the
whole kingdom?" she said.

King Merry nodded unhappily. "I don't
know what to do."

"What about the spellbook?" Ellie
asked.

King Merry stared at the book, then
tucked it back into his robe. "This old
book is very powerful, but it can't be
used very often. It'll be many years
before its magic is recharged enough

to do another big spell," he said sadly.
"And by that time it'll be too late."

"I could try and help," offered Trixi.

King Merry smiled at her. "Thank
you, Trixi, my dear. You really are
a wonderful royal pixie, but you
know your magic can't break my
sister's powerful spells. Not even Aunt
Maybelle's magic can do that."

"It would have to be very strong magic
indeed," sighed Aunt Maybelle.

*POP!*

A familiar wooden box suddenly
appeared on the floor in front of them.

"The Magic Box!" said Summer.

"How strange!" said King Merry in
surprise. "I wonder why it's here?"

The box opened its lid, revealing the
six compartments inside.

"I think it wants to help us," said Jasmine thoughtfully. "But how?" Her eyes searched the contents. Was there something inside that the box wanted them to use? The weather crystal? The unicorn horn? The magic map? Or maybe... She caught her breath as she suddenly spotted the bag of glitter dust with a crescent shape embroidered on it. Maybe they could use one of the two wish spells they had left!

She took the bag out. "Would the glitter dust in here be powerful enough to wish everything back to normal and stop Queen Malice's spell spreading over the land?"

"There's only one way to find out!" King Merry smiled. "Will you do the honours, girls?"

"Throw the glitter dust into the air and wish as hard as you can," Trixi instructed them.

Nervously, Jasmine took a pinch of glitter dust out of the bag.
She, Summer and Ellie looked at each other.
"Ready?" Jasmine whispered. The others nodded. Jasmine threw the dust up into the air and it sparkled as it fell.
"We wish the Secret Kingdom was back to normal!" they all shouted.

There was the brightest golden flash and suddenly everything changed.
The mud and mess disappeared, everyone's rags changed back to ball clothes, the swamp vanished and the

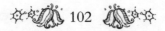

throne transformed. The crystals on
the chandeliers sparkled and the tables
were once more covered with delicious-
looking food arranged on snowy-white
tablecloths. The golden window frames
glittered and twinkle-twinkle bunting
and flower garlands decorated the
ballroom.

"It's worked!" gasped Jasmine,
looking out of the window and seeing
the gardens looking beautiful in the
moonlight.

Everyone started cheering and hugging
each other.

"Everything is just as it should be!" said
King Merry in delight. "Oh, well done!"

The girls helped him to his golden
throne. King Merry held his hands up
high. "Now, let the Summer Ball begin!"

# The Summer Ball

The brownie band started playing as the Summer Ball began. The elves handed out delicious glasses of sparkling fruit punch and people started to help themselves to biscuits, cakes, jellies and frosted fruit. Pixies flew about overhead and elves and imps waltzed each other round. King Merry was too tired to dance but he conducted the music from his throne, a beaming smile on his face – a beam that grew even wider when Bobbins brought him a marshmallow cake on a golden plate.

"It wasn't brought into the palace by a suspicious-looking figure in a hooded cloak, was it?" Jasmine said with a grin.

"Oh, no. I made this one all myself, I promise," said Bobbins with a smile and a bow. He presented King Merry with a golden spoon and King Merry dug in.

"Delicious!" he declared. "Just… *RIBBIT!*"

The girls caught their breath in horror. King Merry's eyes twinkled at them. "Only joking!" he chuckled.

Ellie, Summer and Jasmine let out relieved sighs.

"Oh, what a fabulous ball this is!" said King Merry.

"It's almost perfect," agreed Jasmine.

"*Almost?*" King Merry frowned at her over his spectacles.

"Well, the dancing's a bit old-fashioned," Jasmine said, grinning. "We could always teach everyone some new steps, King Merry!"

"Oh, yes! Please do, my dear!" said King Merry in delight.

Jasmine ran over and jumped onto the stage. Soon she had everyone's attention. "Ellie, Summer and I are going to show you some new dance moves from our world. We'll show you all what to do and you can copy us!" She beckoned the others up. Ellie bounced up but Summer hung back, blushing.

Trixi swooped up beside her. "What's the matter?"

"I can't do it," Summer whispered. "I can't stand on stage in front of everyone."

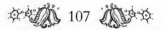

Trixi giggled. "Summer! You managed to defeat Queen Malice! If you can do that, you can do *anything*!"

Summer looked at the little pixie and suddenly realised she was right. She followed the others and faced the guests. They were all looking expectantly at the three girls. *I can do this*, Summer thought.

"Right, this is how it goes," Jasmine instructed. "You clap to the left and then to the right, do a twirl and wiggle then swing each other round!" She demonstrated and Ellie and Summer joined in.

Soon everyone was copying the girls. The brownies started playing a tune that fitted with the dance. When everyone had the hang of the steps the band

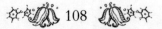

started to play faster and faster until everyone was spinning each other round at top speed. They all finished the dance with pink cheeks and shining eyes. Even Summer had to admit she had loved it!

"That was delightful!" declared King Merry as the girls made their way back to him. Just then the brownies started to play a fanfare, and Trixi twirled her leaf in excitement. "It's almost midnight!" she squealed. "Really this time!"

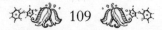

"Everyone hold hands," King Merry commanded, jumping up from his throne. The girls grabbed onto each other, and everyone in the ballroom stood in a circle together while the band counted down. "Five, four, three, two, one… hooray!" everyone cried. As the clock struck midnight, all the pixies tapped their rings and brightly coloured confetti fluttered down from the ceiling.

The brownie band started playing a happy jig, but King Merry yawned deeply. The girls helped him over to his throne. "My, my," the kindly king smiled. "I'm so glad things are right in my kingdom again, but it is rather past my bedtime."

Jasmine sighed happily. "We've had a really amazing time in the Secret

Kingdom, King Merry!"

Summer felt suddenly worried. "Now Queen Malice has been stopped and sent away, we will be able to come back here, won't we?"

"Oh, yes," King Merry said seriously. "My sister may have been stopped for now, but if I know her I'm sure she'll soon be hatching another wicked plan to make me and everyone else in the Secret Kingdom unhappy. Still," he said, smiling at them, "with you to help us, we'll manage to stop her."

"Always!" Jasmine said firmly.

"We'll come as soon as you call us," said Ellie.

"You know you can count on us!" Summer told him.

"I do indeed, my dears." King Merry

yawned again. "I am ever so glad the Magic Box found you. I couldn't have asked for three cleverer, braver people to help keep my kingdom safe. The Magic Box really was one of my best ever inventions, wasn't it, Trixi?"

"Oh, yes, Your Majesty," Trixi nodded. "It…"

A loud snore interrupted her. The king's eyes had shut and he had fallen fast asleep!

Trixi tapped her pixie ring and conjured up a stripy purple-and-white nightcap. She put it carefully on the king's head and then magicked up a fluffy purple blanket.

"Goodnight, King Merry," Summer whispered, helping to tuck it round the kindly little king.

"We'll see you soon," said Jasmine.

"I think I'd better take you home, girls." Trixi told them softly. "Thank you for helping me save the king and the land. You really are wonderful! I hope I see you again soon."

She kissed them all on their noses and then tapped her ring. A cloud of sparkles rushed around them and they felt themselves being lifted into the air. "Bye, Trixi!" they gasped as they were whisked away.

They landed safely back in Jasmine's fortune-telling tent, the Magic Box between them. Outside they could hear the shouts and laughter of the fete. As always, no time had passed since they had left. Summer blinked. "Oh, wow. It feels really strange to be back here."

"Very weird," Ellie agreed as they got to their feet. "But at least we've come back to something fun!"

Jasmine picked up her fortune-teller's scarf from the table and smiled. "I was right. We *did* all have an adventure to go on in a faraway land."

"So what can Madame Jasmina see next for us?" Summer asked, putting the box back into Jasmine's bag.

"Ah, now that is a very good question. Let me see, my dear," said Jasmine, putting on her quavery voice. She took Summer's hand. "Oh, yes! Looking at this hand I see *lots* more adventures!"

"Exciting ones?" said Summer.

"Of course!" Jasmine grinned.

"You know, I can look into the future too." Ellie's eyes twinkled. "And you

 114

know what I can see?"

"What?" Jasmine and Summer asked.

"Lots of cakes!" Ellie opened the tent entrance, letting in the sunshine. "Last one to the cake stall's a stink toad!"

"Ribbit!" said Summer, following her.

Jasmine picked up the bag with the Magic Box in and ran out happily after her friends into the sunshine.

In the next Secret Kingdom
adventure, Ellie, Summer and
Jasmine visit

# Dolphin Bay

**Read on for a sneak peek...**

## A Camping Trip

"Ouch!" squeaked Summer as Ellie
accidentally jabbed her arm with a
plastic spade.

"Sorry!" Ellie tucked the spade between
a stripy beach ball and the picnic hamper,
which was squashed against her legs
on the floor of the car. "I was trying to
get the sweets. Who wants a strawberry
sherbet?"

"Me, please!" Summer and Jasmine chorused together.

"Us too," said Molly, Ellie's little sister. "Don't we, Caitlin?"

Ellie leaned forward to offer Molly and her friend the packet, then passed them to Summer and Jasmine, who were sitting on either side of her.

"How ever did you manage to find them amongst all our stuff?" asked Jasmine, taking two sweets from the bag. Every centimetre of the people carrier was jam-packed with holiday things. There were rucksacks, bright orange tents, snuggly sleeping bags, a tiny cooking stove, plastic spades and fishing nets. Ellie's parents were taking Ellie, her best friends Summer and Jasmine, and Molly and her friend Caitlin on a camping holiday by the seaside for a whole week.

"It was a tough job, but someone had to do it." Ellie grinned.

"How much further is it, Dad?" Molly sighed.

"Not long now," said Mr Macdonald. "Look out for the signs to the campsite."

"I wonder what it'll be like?" Summer pushed her long blonde plaits back over her shoulders. "Do you think we'll see dolphins swimming in the sea?"

"If we don't see dolphins then I'll make you a sand one," promised Ellie. Her green eyes sparkled with excitement. "I'll decorate it with shells and seaweed."

There was a far away look on Jasmine's face. "I love the beach. It's like an enormous stage. I'm going to practise my new dance steps on it."

"We're going to have a brilliant time!" declared Ellie happily.

"Maybe even a magic time!" whispered Jasmine with a grin. She caught her friends' eyes. The three of them had an exciting secret. They looked after a magical box that had been made by the kindly King Merry, who was the ruler of an enchanted land called the Secret Kingdom. The Secret Kingdom was a very special place, where amazing creatures like pixies, elves and unicorns lived. Whenever there was trouble in the Secret Kingdom a message appeared in the Magic Box and Ellie, Summer and Jasmine were whisked away to the kingdom to try and help. Usually it was because King Merry's horrible sister, Queen Malice, had been causing problems.

Suddenly Molly squealed. "I see a sign!"

"Sunny Sands Campsite!" Ellie read out. "We're here!"

The moment Mr Macdonald stopped the car and switched off the engine, Ellie, Summer and Jasmine unbuckled their seat belts and tumbled out. At the bottom of the hill was a hedge and beyond the hedge was the glittering blue sea!

"Look at the sea!" Jasmine cried. "It's beautiful." She twirled round on the grass, her long dark hair swinging around her. "This is so exciting."

"What can we do to help, Mrs Macdonald?" Summer asked. Molly and Caitlin had already run over to a patch of grass and were doing cartwheels and handstands.

"Should we start getting the tents out?" said Ellie. She opened the car boot and immediately a jumble of bags fell out. "Whoops!"

Summer and Jasmine quickly picked the bags up.

"Maybe Dad and I would be better sorting everything out on our own," said Ellie's mum. "Why don't you three just go and explore? The beach is on the other side of that hedge, but keep away from the water."

"Okay, thanks, Mum!" Ellie said.

"Race you both to the beach!" called Jasmine.

Ellie and Summer tore after her as she ran towards a gap in the hedge. They caught up with her and stepped onto the beach together.

"Isn't the sea beautiful,' said Ellie, looking at the waves lapping at the shore. "I want to get my paints out and paint a picture of it."

Jasmine twirled her round and laughed. "This is going to be the best holiday ever!"

Summer's sandals sunk into the soft sand and she sighed happily. "The sand's almost as pretty as the sand on Glitter Beach in the Secret Kingdom."

"Only this sand won't turn into magical dust!" said Ellie, thinking of Glitter Beach with its aquamarine sea, golden sand and little fairy shops surrounding it.

"Where's the Magic Box at the moment?" Jasmine asked curiously.

"In my rucksack back at the car," Ellie replied. Excitement tingled through her.

She hoped they would be needed soon.
She couldn't wait to visit the Secret
Kingdom again.

Read

# Dolphin Bay

to find out what
happens next!

Enjoy six sparkling adventures.
Collect them all!

Out now!

# Secret Kingdom

A magical world of
friendship and fun!

Join best friends
Ellie, Summer and Jasmine at

www.secretkingdombooks.com

and enjoy games, sneak peeks
and lots more!

You'll find great activities, competitions, stories
and games, plus a special newsletter for
Secret Kingdom friends!

# Secret Kingdom Codebreaker

Sssh! Can you keep a secret? Ellie, Summer and Jasmine have written a new special message just for you! They have written one secret word of their special message in each of the six Secret Kingdom books in series two. To discover the secret word, hold a small mirror to this page and see your word magically appear!

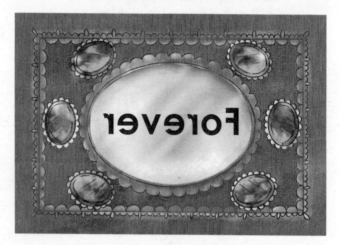

## The sixth secret word is: _____

When you have cracked the code and found all six secret words,
work out the special message and go online to enter the competition at

## www.secretkingdombooks.com

We will put all of the correct entries into a draw and select one winner to receive a special Secret Kingdom goody bag featuring lots of sparkly gifts, including a glittery t-shirt!

You can also send your entry on a postcard to:

Secret Kingdom Competition, Orchard Books, 338 Euston Road, London, NW1 3I

Don't forget to include your name and address.

## Good luck!

Closing Date: 31st July 2013.

# Collect the tokens from each Secret Kingdom book to get special Secret Kingdom gifts!

In every Secret Kingdom book there are three Friendship Tokens that you can exchange for special gifts! Send your friendship tokens in to us as soon as you get them or save them up to get an even more special gift!

**3** tokens

Secret Kingdom poster and collectable glittery bookmark

**6** tokens

Scrummy scented stickers

**8** tokens

Secret Kingdom pen

**15** tokens

Glittery t-shirt

**18** tokens

Secret Kingdom pink cap

To take part in this offer, please send us a letter telling us why you like Secret Kingdom. Don't forget to:
1) Tell us which gift you would like to exchange your tokens for
2) Include the correct number of Friendship Tokens for each gift you are requesting
3) Include your name and address
4) Include the signature of a parent or guardian

Secret Kingdom Friendship Token Offer
Orchard Books Marketing Department
338 Euston Road, London, NW1 3BH

### Closing date: 31st May 2013

### www.secretkingdombooks.com

1 Friendship Token
www.secretkingdombooks.com

1 Friendship Token
www.secretkingdombooks.com

1 Friendship Token
www.secretkingdombooks.com

# Secret Kingdom

Look out for the next sparkling
summer special!

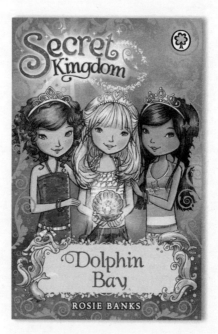

Available
June 2013